Fireflies

Alice Hoffman

Illustrated by
Wayne McLoughlin

Hyperion Books for Children
New York

Once there was a village that was covered with snow from November until May. Because winter lasted so long, and because there was a wide and beautiful river at the edge of town, all the children were excellent ice-skaters. Even the babies were taught to skate as soon as they could walk. No one here minded snow or ice or the frost that formed on every window. Winter, after all, was followed by spring. On that they could always depend.

Every year, on the first of May, the fireflies would return from the other side of the Yellow Mountains. They would appear all at once, in a shining cloud that rose above the rooftops and the trees. Beneath the light of the fireflies, the snow in the meadows would vanish. Crocuses and violets would sprout in the grass. A festival was always held on this night, to celebrate the end of winter. A band would play, and mothers and fathers would dance, and all around the bandstand the paper lanterns would glow with yellow light as fireflies clustered inside.

But this year something had gone wrong. It was already the middle of May and the fireflies hadn't returned. Chickens laid eggs that were encased in blocks of ice. Little lambs peered out of their barns and cried to see fields of snow. Laundry hanging out to dry on the line turned into icicles shaped like table-cloths and pajamas and socks.

The grown-ups wondered if they would ever again see their fields of hay and their gardens bursting with vegetables. Every day there was less food in the pantries, less hay in the barns.

Only the children weren't upset by a world that was
all snow and ice. Now they could skate as long as they
wanted at the river. And that's exactly what they did,
except for Jackie Healy, who was the worst skater for
miles around.

Jackie didn't glide across the ice like other children.
He slipped and slopped, flipped and flopped. He
crashed into neighbors and trees. One winter he
sprained his ankle just by trying to stop. People teased
him that he was too clumsy to lace up his skates. They
laughed when they saw him coming, tripping over his
own big feet.

Jackie was a sweet boy, and his mother and father loved him. They didn't care if he ever learned to skate. They didn't mind if the dishes rattled every time he closed the door or if every ball he threw shattered the window in the front hall. They knew he didn't mean to break the eggs he collected from the henhouse or tear his new clothes as soon as he put them on. The important thing was that Jackie always tried his best.

But Jackie felt that he had failed his parents—and failed himself as well. Now, during this long winter when the fireflies didn't return, Jackie came up with a plan he hoped would change everything. Each night, after supper, he took his skates down to a part of the river that was hidden by reeds. Here, no one would see when he tripped over stones or slipped on the slick blue ice.

For hours each night, he skidded along the river. He worked so hard to improve his skating that he soon had blisters on all of his toes. He kept graham crackers in his pockets, for extra energy, and he wore two pairs of gloves, to make certain his fingers wouldn't freeze. He skated for so many hours that the rabbits who lived in the reeds grew to recognize him. The fish who swam beneath the ice no longer darted away.

Yet no matter how hard he practiced, Jackie could barely stand upright. One night a gang of older boys hid in the reeds to watch him. They laughed and tossed rocks in his path. Even then, Jackie kept practicing. Or at least he tried. His right foot tripped over his left foot, and before he could stop himself, Jackie was sprawled out in front of the biggest, meanest boy in town.

"You are pathetic," the boy told Jackie. "I'll bet your own family doesn't want to admit you belong to them."

Jackie had often wondered if his parents wished they had a different son. The sort of boy who could skate in a perfect circle and climb trees without falling and pitch a ball without breaking a window. Maybe it would be better if he disappeared. Without saying a word, without thinking twice, Jackie ran off toward the Yellow Mountains, where no one would find him.

"Go on," the boys at the riverbank shouted after him. "Good riddance," they called, sure that Jackie would soon head for home.

But in the morning, Jackie Healy was nowhere to be found. His mother cried hundreds of tears when she saw his empty bed. Then she called to Jackie's father, who gathered together everyone in the town.

They all went to look for Jackie. They searched the barns and the school yard and along the riverbank. They looked all through the day, and then all night as well. At last, a little girl found Jackie's skates, which he had thrown away at the foot of the mountain. Everyone knew this was not a good sign. They turned to look at the mountains. In a winter as cold as this one, who could survive in those woods? It was so cold, the bears were still asleep in their dens, hugging themselves for warmth. So cold, the owls froze to the trees.

Jackie hadn't thought about the cold when he ran away. He had run so fast and so far that by the time he had stopped crying and realized he wanted to go home, he was already lost. He tried his best to backtrack. He made his way through the brambles until at last he found a footprint. To his surprise, it was the same size as his own. As a matter of fact, it *was* his own. He'd been going around in circles, and was just as far from home as ever.

Jackie Healy might have frozen to the spot where he stood, without any hope of ever leaving the Yellow Mountains, if he'd been the sort of boy who could skate in perfect circles or climb a tree or pitch a ball without breaking windows. But Jackie was still himself, and when he tried to lean against a tree he missed it entirely.

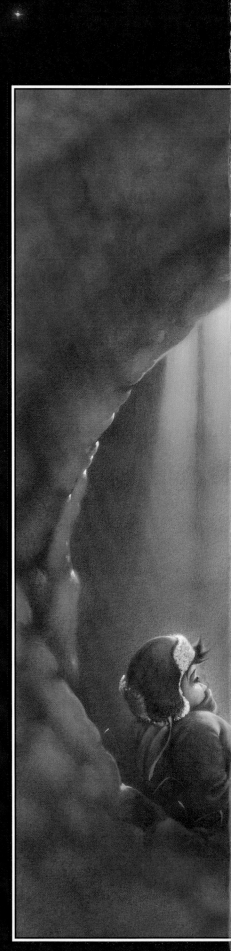

He fell to the ground, and to his surprise, he just kept falling. He had stumbled into a cave. Down he went, and down some more, until at last he crashed to a stop. Jackie was so exhausted and grateful for a place to rest he didn't even wonder why the cave was so warm and soft. He slept the whole night through, and when he awoke he discovered that an orphan wolf pup was curled up right beside him.

A boy who could skate in perfect circles would have jumped to his feet. That kind of boy would have climbed out of the cave and run away. But when Jackie tried to get up, the sleeve of his coat caught on a rock. When he tried to climb, he fell backward.

I'm done for, Jackie thought as the wolf came to sit on his chest.

Jackie closed his eyes and waited for something awful to happen. But the wolf only licked his face, then nosed in his pockets for crumbs. Jackie sat up, reached deep into his pocket, and pulled out a graham cracker. The pup was so hungry it gobbled every bit.

From then on the wolf refused to leave Jackie's side. After bounding out of the cave with one leap, the pup waited politely while Jackie pulled himself up.

Once back on open ground, Jackie patted the wolf, said good-bye, then started on his way. But when Jackie stopped, confused about which way was east and which way west, there was the wolf, right beside him.

"Stay," Jackie commanded.

But of course, the wolf wouldn't listen. It trailed along until Jackie gave in, and that didn't take long. The truth was, Jackie liked the company.

"You're like my shadow," Jackie said, and that was what he decided to call the pup.

Together, Jackie and Shadow made their way through the Yellow Mountains. Jackie tried not to think about the cold. He tried not to think about how hungry he felt or how scared he was of the dark.

The next evening, just as the sky was turning purple, Shadow tilted his head. The wolf jumped in front of Jackie; his fur stood on end. Something was moving in the bushes, something that growled and broke branches with every step.

Out came a bear that had been sleeping all winter long. Hunger had woken the bear and now it was so starved it licked its lips at the sight of anything that might be dinner—which, at that moment, happened to be Jackie and Shadow.

Shadow howled, but what could a small wolf do? It was up to Jackie to defend them, so he reached down and grabbed a rock.

"Don't come any closer," he told the bear.

The bear growled and took another step.

If Jackie had been the sort of boy who could pitch a ball without breaking windows, he would have hit his mark when he threw the rock. But Jackie was

still himself, and his aim was so wild, he missed the bear completely. Instead, the rock struck a pine tree where bees had stored the best of last season's honey. The thump shook the tree and every bit of honey spilled out. If a bear could smile, then this one did. There were gallons of honey, so much that after the bear had eaten its fill, Jackie and Shadow had plenty for their dinner as well.

That night the boy and wolf slept curled together in a badger's burrow they found when Jackie tripped over it. Beneath a blanket of brown leaves, Jackie thought about his mother, who never complained when he broke her favorite teacups or tore his new clothes. He thought of his father, who was never angry when Jackie knocked the board over in the middle of a game of checkers. He realized how worried his parents must be, and he grew even more determined to find his way back.

But after walking all the next day, Jackie was still no closer to home. He decided to climb a tree in the hopes of sighting his village. If he had been the sort of boy who could climb with ease, he could have looked over the mountains and seen the smoke streaming out of his very own chimney. But Jackie was still himself, and when he tried to shinny up a tree, his hands slipped on the smooth bark and he crashed onto a ledge of a gray rock. He fell so hard that the rock trembled and quaked, then flew skyward.

As soon as Jackie was back on solid ground, Shadow ran to lick his face. Jackie was fine, but he did feel something very strange. Something was tickling his palm. From between his fingers a faint yellow light glowed. Slowly, carefully, Jackie opened his hand.

A firefly rose into the air, past the trees, higher and higher, until it joined the cloud of thousands of its sisters and brothers. All winter long, the fireflies had been trapped beneath the rock. Jackie went to peer over the edge of the hole. The light from inside was so blinding, he had to squint. More and more fireflies rose out of the earth. There were fireflies in Shadow's fur and in the pockets of Jackie's coat. There were fireflies above them and under them and on every side. Fireflies formed a single shining stream of light, following the same route they took every year. Through the Yellow Mountains, toward home.

A little girl in the village was the first to see them. "They've come back!" she shouted when she saw the glow of yellow light.

The grown-ups were so grumpy and cold they might never have paid attention, but all at once the snow began to melt, as it did every year on the night of the fireflies' return. Ice thawed. Grass turned green. New strawberries, which had been ripening under the snowdrifts, were already juicy and red.

Jackie's mother stood where she was and blinked. A pup the color of moonlight trotted along the road that led out of the woods, and beside it strode a boy who was grinning and waving and tripping over his own feet.

"It's Jackie!" his mother cried.

And there he was, surrounded by winking globes of light. There were fireflies inside his shirt, and even his boots glowed with light. Jackie had come back from the mountains with summer in his pockets.

Every neighbor in the village called out Jackie's name. Everyone applauded and wanted to shake his hand. His mother and father ran to him and kissed him, and the mayor declared that Jackie had rescued them all.

At last, the festival to celebrate the end of winter could be held. Up on the bandstand, Jackie was presented with the blue ribbon of courage, and the red ribbon of loyalty was tied around Shadow's neck. Boys and girls came to pet the pup who had followed Jackie home, and if any of the grown-ups observed that Shadow looked like a wolf, with moonlit fur and yellow eyes, they didn't mention it.

And now every winter, from November until May, the children continue to skate along the river. Some boys and girls spin and glide, some stumble and fall, but they all wave when they see Jackie and Shadow walking through the woods. Now nobody notices whether or not Jackie Healy still trips over his own feet. In this village, nobody cares about that sort of thing anymore.

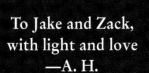

To Jake and Zack,
with light and love
—A. H.

For the boys and girls of Bellows Falls, Vermont,
children of the river
—W. McL.

Text © 1997 by Alice Hoffman.
Illustrations © 1997 by Wayne McLoughlin.

Printed in the United States of America.

First Edition
1 3 5 7 9 10 8 6 4 2

The artwork for each picture is prepared using acrylic and pencil on bristol board.
This book is set in 12-point Stemple Garamond.
Designed by Stephanie Bart-Horvath.

Library of Congress Cataloging-in-Publication Data
Hoffman, Alice.
Fireflies/Alice Hoffman; illustrated by Wayne McLoughlin.
p.   cm.
Summary: Jackie can't run and skate and throw as well as the other children, but
his clumsiness eventually saves the villagers from a winter that would not end.
ISBN 0-7868-0227-8 (trade)—ISBN 0-7868-2180-9 (lib. bdg.)
[1. Clumsiness—Fiction. 2. Winter—Fiction. 3. Fireflies—Fiction.] I. McLoughlin,
Wayne, ill. II. Title.
PZ7.H67445Fi 1997
[Fic]—dc20   96-42232